© 2011 Disney Enterprises, Inc.
Published by Hachette Partworks Ltd
ISBN: 978-1-906965-37-2
Date of Printing: February 2011
Printed in Singapore by Tien Wah Press

DINOSAUR

Disney

Hachette

Long ago in a forgotten time, mighty dinosaurs roamed the Earth. These dinosaurs lived off the lush, beautiful land and dwelled in harmony with each other.

One day, an enemy carnotaur, looking for food, invaded a peaceful colony of iguanodons.

A mother iguanodon quickly gathered up the eggs from her nest and protected them from the carnotaur. But one of the eggs was left behind.

The egg was about to begin an amazing journey! First, it was snatched by a hungry lizard, who accidentally dropped it into a river. The egg floated downstream and was eventually snatched up by a pteranodon. This huge flying creature carried it across a wide sea.

The pteranodon finally dropped the egg as it was flying above a small island. Luckily, the egg landed gently on a pile of soft leaves.

A small, furry lemur called Plio found the egg amongst the leaves. As she approached it – CRACK! – the shell of the egg split open and a strange-looking creature emerged.

"Dad, get over here!" she cried, as she cradled the iguanodon in her arms.

Plio's father, Yar, cautiously came near, followed by a young lemur called Zini.

"It's a cold-blooded monster from across the sea," said Yar. "That thing is dangerous! Get rid of it!"

But as Plio tenderly held the happy baby, her heart opened up to him. She knew he was lost and alone. Even Yar had to admit that the cute little orphan needed a home.

So in the end, they decided that the baby iguanodon would become a member of their family.

The lemurs named the baby Aladar. He grew up to be big and strong.

Despite his large size, Aladar loved to play with his lemur friends, especially Plio's daughter, Suri.

One day, Suri and her friends shrieked with delight as they raced through the trees, with Aladar chasing them.

"Oh no!" Aladar jokingly cried when he caught up with them. "Attacking lemurs!" They all jumped on Aladar and started tickling him until he couldn't take it any more.

"OK, you got me!" laughed the ticklish dinosaur. "Come on, pick on someone your own size!"

Plio interrupted their game.

"All right, guys, break it up," she said. "Remember the Courtship? You're going to miss all that smooching."

The Courtship was a yearly ceremony when the young lemurs chose their mates.

"Go find Zini," said Plio, smiling at Aladar. "He's rehearsing his pick-up lines somewhere."

Aladar found Zini at the beach, practising
his lines. Zini was sure that he would be able
to attract a mate.

But when he arrived at the Ritual Tree for
the ceremony, he got tangled up in the vines
and missed all the action. By the end of the
ceremony, Zini was the only lemur without
a mate.

Aladar knew how Zini felt. As the only iguanodon on the small island, Aladar wondered whether he himself would ever find a mate.

"Don't worry, Zini," said Aladar, trying to cheer his friend up. "You always have next year."

Suddenly, bright lights started flashing in the night sky. All the lemurs looked up in amazement.

"Aladar, where's Suri?" asked Plio. She knew something was terribly wrong.

A huge meteor shower was falling to Earth. The power of it hitting the ground caused a huge ball of fire. It was heading straight for the island!

Aladar found Suri. He placed her
and Plio on his back, then Yar and Zini
jumped on. With his family clinging on,
Aladar ran to escape the flames, which
were fast catching up with them.

"Run, Aladar, run!" shouted Plio.

With the flames at his tail, Aladar
jumped into the sea and carried everyone
to safety on the mainland.

Sadly, Lemur Island was destroyed.
Aladar and his lemur family would have
to find a new home.

It was a hard journey. There was no food or water.
But the brave group continued, full of hope.

Suddenly, the ground began to shake. A huge
dust-storm was approaching. Before they knew it,
they were surrounded by a herd of dinosaurs!

"Stay out of my way!" roared Kron, the leader of the herd, as he marched past the group.

"You heard Kron! Move it!" added Bruton, Kron's lieutenant.

Aladar and the others were amazed.

"Look at all the Aladars!" gasped Suri.

After the main part of the herd had rushed
through, a small group of dinosaurs slowly followed
behind.

"My name is Aladar," the iguanodon greeted them.
"This is my family."

Aladar's new friends were Baylene, an enormous
brachiosaur, Eema the styracosaur and Url, a little
ankylosaur.

Aladar learned from them that the herd was on its way to a place called the Nesting Grounds.

"It is the most beautiful place there is, child," Eema explained. "It's where the herd goes to have their babies."

Because of the meteor, the journey was even more difficult than usual. And Kron was moving the herd along very fast.

"We can hardly keep up," complained Baylene.

Aladar wanted to help his new friends, so he ran ahead to speak to Kron. He explained that Eema and Baylene were having a hard time keeping up with the herd.

"So you know, Kron," said Aladar, "maybe you could slow it down a bit?"

But Kron didn't seem to care about Eema and Baylene. He believed that only the strongest deserved to survive.

After Kron stormed off, his sister, Neera, walked up to Aladar.

"Don't worry," she said, smiling. "That's how my brother treats newcomers — no matter how charming they are."

Aladar watched Neera as she walked away. He wondered whether her smile was for him.

The next morning, the herd set off for a lake. To reach it, they would have to cross a large desert.

Kron told Bruton to instruct the newcomers.

"Listen up," Bruton yelled. "There is no water until the other side. If a predator catches you, you're on your own!"

At last, the herd arrived at the lake. But there wasn't any water in it!

Eema was ready to cry. "There has always been water here before," she wailed.

Kron realised that the explosion from the meteor shower must have dried up the lake. He ordered the herd to keep moving.

But Eema was exhausted. She couldn't go on.

"Oh, Eema, please!" begged Baylene. "The herd won't wait. We must carry on."

Baylene stepped forward. As she did, her foot made a *squishing* sound. Her enormous brachiosaurus foot had sunk so deep into the ground that it had hit water!

Aladar called out to the rest of the herd:

"Water! Come on!"

Later, Aladar told Neera that he thought the herd should be kinder to its weaker members.

"Everyone counts," Aladar explained. "If we watch out for each other, we all stand a better chance of getting to your Nesting Grounds."

Neera was surprised to hear Aladar speak so strongly. She had never met anyone with such compassion before.

Meanwhile, Kron watched Neera and Aladar from a nearby hill. Seeing his sister and the newcomer together made him angry!

Suddenly, a voice cried out in pain. "Kron!"

Kron turned to see Bruton, badly hurt. When Kron asked Bruton who had hurt him, Bruton gasped, "The carnotaurs!"

"They never come this far north," said Kron.

"The fireball must have driven them out," replied Bruton.

They had to escape from their predators. Kron
ordered the herd to move out quickly.

Aladar wanted to be close to Neera at the front,
but he also felt responsible for his friends, who were
trailing at the back of the herd.

"Come on you guys," he urged. "We're going to be
left behind!"

But Aladar's friends just couldn't keep up.

A thunderstorm moved in. As lightning flashed
and thunder roared, the little group of stragglers
got lost.

Then a shadowy figure appeared in the distance.
Was it an enemy carnotaur?

"Oh, it's Bruton!" cried Eema.

Bruton looked badly hurt. Aladar offered to help him, but Bruton refused.

Just then, a flash of lightning lit up the sky. Aladar saw that Eema's pet, Url, had discovered the entrance to some caves.

"If you change your mind," said Aladar to Bruton, "we'll be in those caves."

Soon, Bruton did change his mind. He followed the others into the cave.

Inside the cave, Plio tended to Bruton's wounds. Bruton noticed that Aladar was talking encouragingly to the others.

"Why is he doing this, pushing them on with false hope?" Bruton asked Plio.

"It's hope that has got us this far," Plio explained.

Later that night, as everyone slept peacefully,
the carnotaurs found the cave.

"I'll hold them off!" Bruton yelled to Aladar.
"You help the others!"

Bruton bravely held back the terrible carnotaurs.
Aladar led the others deep into the cave.

To stop the carnotaurs getting in, Bruton
knocked down a pillar to cause a landslide. But the
rocks fell on him.

The carnotaurs were beaten. But the way out of the cave was now blocked. Aladar and the others went deeper into the cave, desperately searching for an exit.

"Hold on a minute," Zini said, sniffing the air. "Do you smell that?"

"Yeah!" answered Suri. It was fresh air.

They soon found a small gap in the rocks. A ray of sunshine shone through it.

"Everybody stand back!" Aladar shouted, throwing himself at the rock wall. But a small landslide blocked out the ray of light from outside.

Losing hope, Aladar said, "We're not meant to survive."

"Shame on you," Baylene scolded him. "You allowed an old fool like me to believe I was needed. And do you know what? You were right!"

With their last ounce of strength everyone rammed the rock wall together until – CRASH! – they finally broke through. And there, in front of them, were the Nesting Grounds!

Eema and Aladar
noticed that the main route
to the Nesting Grounds was blocked by a
mountain of boulders. Aladar thought of Neera
and the rest of the herd.

"They'll never make it over that," Aladar said.
He raced back through the cave to tell them
of the secret way to the Nesting Grounds.

Aladar found Kron trying to make the herd go up and over the dangerous rockfall.

"Stop!" Aladar cried. "I've been to the Nesting Grounds. There's a safer way."

Neera tried to persuade her brother to listen to Aladar. But Kron was furious. Aladar was challenging his leadership. Kron charged at Aladar and knocked him to the ground.

Suddenly, a mighty sound thundered out – *ROAR*!
It was a carnotaur! The herd panicked and began to
run away.

"No, don't move!" Aladar told them. "If we scatter,
the carnotaur will pick us off one by one. Stand
together!"

The herd joined Aladar. Side by side, they bravely
stood up to the carnotaur.

But suddenly, the carnotaur saw the one member who stood alone – Kron.

The carnotaur charged. Aladar and Neera rushed to help Kron, but they were too late. Kron fell to the ground.

With strength, courage and Neera's help, Aladar defeated the carnotaur. The herd cheered wildly.

Then Aladar led everyone to the Nesting Grounds. With Neera by his side, Aladar declared proudly, "Welcome home!"

Weeks later, everyone gathered to see a joyful event. A tiny egg cracked open. A beautiful baby iguanodon was born.

"He looks just like me," Aladar announced.

"Meet your dad," Neera said, smiling at her newborn. "He's not as crazy as he looks." Everyone laughed.

At long last, the lemurs and Aladar had found a wonderful new home.

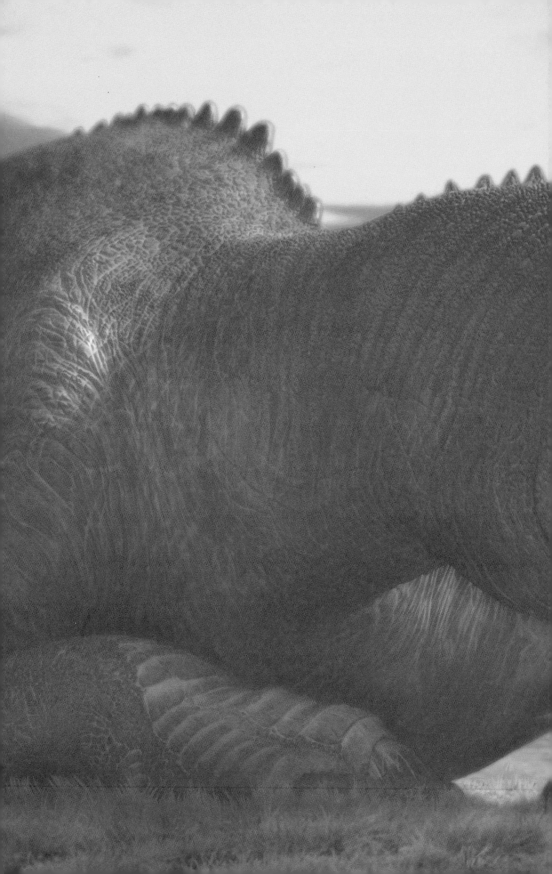